Visit

WWW.YOUNGERMEACADEMY.COM

to request an author visit for your organization, download free coloring pages, watch free video e-books, and more.

If you enjoy this book, please

LEAVE A REVIEW →

to support our independent family project.

Created by Ben Okon

Illustrated by Jeevankar Bansiwal

For my son Judah, a curious problem solver who can't wait to try again

Special thanks to my mom, who taught me to believe that
every problem has a solution

Published by Younger Media, LLC

www.youngermeacademy.com

ISBN: 978-1-961428-00-3 (hardcover)

Library of Congress Control Number: 2023910783

Hardcover edition manufactured in China.

Judah Giraffe was out having a laugh,
playing Jungle Ball—leading his team.
He stretched his neck tall to headbutt the ball . . .
when he suddenly heard a scared scream.

"Hey there, Judah, look out!" he could hear a bird shout.
Teddy Toucan flew towards him with haste.
"The whole river is dry!" Teddy yelled from up high.
"So it's clear we have no time to waste!"

"I have asked all around! There's no drink to be found,"
Teddy huffed, out of breath, to his friend.
"Now, what else can we do? We can't all drink the dew!
I don't like where this story might end!"

"My, oh my," Judah said as he tilted his head.
"Yes, we sure need an answer, but how?
Instead of just crying, let's both begin trying
to form a hypothesis now."

"Hypo-what?" Teddy cried with his eyes open wide.
"Hey, just hearing that word gives me stress!"

Judah said, "Don't get queasy. You'll see, it's quite easy . . .
it means that we'll take our best guess."

"Really—how could that help?" Teddy asked with a yelp.
"Any guess wouldn't give us a shot!"

Judah answered, "Not true, and I'll prove it to you.
'Cause a guess could accomplish a lot!"

"When a challenge or query is making you weary,
and answers are not in a book,
you can worry for years, crying oceans of tears . . .
or else, guess, and have somewhere to look!"

"But a guess can be wrong, and we don't have too long!"
Teddy cautioned his friend as he flew.

Judah said, "What's the harm? There's no cause for alarm.
If we're wrong, we can try something new!
Now, the stream could be blocked, and I wouldn't be shocked.
Or perhaps, it was drained, dried, or sunk."

"That could be," muttered Teddy, "'cause Elephant Eddie
likes drinking it up with his trunk!"

They moved out to the shade, where the elephants played,
and saw Eddie was suffering thirst.
Teddy, shaking his head, cried, "I meant what I said!
Guessing answers is simply the worst!"

"Wait a sec—think it through! We just learned something new,"
Judah said. "We've become quite a pair!
We can tell no one drank it, so what could have sank it?
Oh, maybe a sinkhole is there!"

"If a hole were that vast, I could find it quite fast!"
Teddy said. "I'll just take a quick glance!"
With his throat feeling dry, Teddy surged towards the sky,
fearing this would provide their last chance.

"Nope, no holes to be seen!" Teddy yelled from the scene.
"But I see a strange hill near the bank!"
As he focused his eyes, he was filled with surprise:
It was clear that no water had sank!

Down to Judah, he squawked: "Look! The river is blocked!
There's a hippo clan—soundly asleep!"

"Hey there, hippos, please wake! It's for all of our sake,
since the river can't run past your heap!"

Said the hippos, "We'll go!" Water started to flow
as they slowly moved off towards the trees.
Barely stopping to think, Teddy took a long drink.
"Thank you, Judah!" he said with more ease.

"My dear friend, you were right!" Teddy squealed with delight
as he flipped and he twirled through the sky.
"There's no purpose in stressing! We could just be guessing,
which offers new things we can try!"

On a jubilant whim, the two went for a swim
and then frolicked and played in the sun.
They renewed their resolve to find problems to solve:
Focused guessing can get the job done!

"OLDER ME" ACADEMY

(More about the Scientific Method for adults and advanced readers)

Have you ever faced a challenge that seemed impossible? Daunting problems can make us lose confidence or feel defensive about our abilities. But confidence doesn't need to come from feeling capable. Instead, it can come from being comfortable with making mistakes or being wrong!

Scientists, for example, are well educated and capable, yet their Scientific Method forces them to assume that they will be wrong. Scientists start by forming a hypothesis, which is an informed guess that is assumed to be incorrect. Then, they use structured testing (read more on this in our book *Nora and Cora Narwhal Prove Whales Can Fly*) to determine if they were right. If they were wrong, they happily improve their guess with what they've learned and test it again. By being willing to be wrong and trying again, their guesses get better over time—that's why science is always improving!

The Scientific Method doesn't need to be used for scientific problems, nor do its 'tests' necessarily need to be rigorous. It works in many everyday situations when you are discovering, creating, or solving something new.

Facing a tough question? Take a guess, and find some evidence to see if you're right. Have writer's block? Write anything down on paper, then take a break and edit it or start again! Inventing a product? Build multiple cheap prototypes, and see which works best! It works in so many places! Just keep a few things in mind:

- **Not everyone thinks this way.** To avoid seeming arrogant or misleading someone who may not understand that you are hypothesizing, caveat your guesses with your level of confidence given your testing, and remain open to the fact that you might be wrong.

- **Beware of confirmation bias.** Our brains are wired to confirm (rather than disprove) what we already think. Actively look for ways to disprove yourself, rather than just trying to convince yourself that you are right.

- **Hypothesize early, before the stakes get high.** You'll almost definitely be wrong a few times before you're right, so leave time to iterate!

- **The rigor of your tests should depend on the importance of the situation.** Scientists test rigorously because their findings can impact the whole world. But when there is less to lose by being wrong, you may not need to worry as much. Sometimes it's just fun to guess!

Hypothesizing can be uncomfortable at first because nobody likes being wrong. But the more you do it, the more comfortable it gets and the better your guesses become. Keep at it, and soon you'll be solving tough problems with ease!

Fun fact: Giraffes can go weeks without drinking water. That helped Judah stay calm even when he was wrong—he hypothesized early, before being right became urgent!

The Story Behind Younger Me Academy

Great children's books create special moments that can be shared across generations.

I realized this when my grandmother Gigi, a retired writing teacher, became isolated during COVID-19 with no way to meet my new baby Judah. Instead, we connected over video, where we enjoyed reading Judah's books together.

These moments we shared—the three of us, across nearly 100 years of age—were special, but usually not because of the books. Most books were written for *Judah* without reaching out to pull *me* into his moment as well. They taught him the ABC's, showed him pictures of new things, and told him stories about sharing and friendship.

But I wanted a book that I could learn from, too. In particular, I wanted to learn things that I wished I had learned when I was younger, so that Judah and I could grow together. I began writing my own books, and the *Younger Me Academy* was born. Each book is designed to:

- **Help anybody of any age learn and grow** with simplified life-long lessons from science, psychology, business, and beyond.

- **Pull everyone in** (including older readers and younger listeners) through vividly illustrated, character-driven stories written with rhythm and rhyme.

- **Create a deep, special moment** between easily-distracted kids and parents with stories that are long enough to savor but short enough to finish in one fun read.

Younger Me Academy is dedicated to Gigi. Through her writing, teaching, and stories, she inspired me to be a better father, husband, friend, professional, and human. My dream is that this series can continue her legacy by helping other growth-oriented families and their "Younger Me's" to do the same.

Thanks for reading. Please support this independent family project by leaving a book review wherever you found *Younger Me Academy.* I love to learn from you too, so I read every single one.

Ben

Ben Okon is a father who never outgrew his childhood habit of asking "why?" and "how?" Now that he has to be the one giving the answers, he loves challenging himself to think through the things he wishes he had known earlier in life from the perspective of a child.

In his spare time, Ben is a business leader who has developed people, product, and corporate strategies with companies like Google, Bain & Co., and Starwood Hotels. He holds an MBA from the Wharton School of Business at the University of Pennsylvania and a BS from the School of Hotel Administration at Cornell University.